HOW TO
SCARE A
GHOST

illustrated by Lee Wildish

by Jean Reagan

Hodder
Children's
Books

For Jane, who always "rocks" Halloween
—J.R.

First published in the United States by Alfred A. Knopf, an imprint
of Random House Children's Books, a division of Random House Inc., New York

First published in the UK in 2018 by Hodder Children's Books

Hodder Children's Books
An imprint of Hachette Children's Group
Part of Hodder & Stoughton
Carmelite House, 50 Victoria Embankment,
London, EC4Y 0DZ

Text copyright © Jean Reagan 2018
Illustrations copyright © Lee Wildish 2018

A CIP catalogue record for this book is available from the British Library

MIX
Paper from
responsible sources
FSC® C104740
FSC
www.fsc.org

ISBN: 978 1 444 93943 9
1 3 5 7 9 10 8 6 4 2

An Hachette UK Company
www.hachette.co.uk
www.hachettechildrens.co.uk

Do you want to scare a ghost? The easiest,
spookiest time to try is . . . Halloween!

First, you have to find one.

HOW TO ATTRACT A GHOST:

*Hide scarecrows in your garden.

No ghost yet? Keep your eyes
wide open while you do more
Halloweeny things – even at school.

GHOSTS CAN'T RESIST:

* Bobbing for apples.

$1+1=2$ $2-1=1$

$2+2=4$ $3-2=1$

HAPPY HALLOWEEN

FLOUR

* Cupcakes.

* Games.

* Glitter.

Still no luck? Don't give up. Try one last trick – MAKE **SCAAAAAAARY** SOUNDS:

✱ A witch's "Heeee

heeee

heeee!"

* An owl's

"Whoo! Whoo!

Whoo! Whoo!"

* And an eerie, ghostly

"Booooooooo!"

Yes! You found one! But is the ghost *real* . . .
or just a kid in a costume?

HOW TO TELL IF A GHOST IS REAL:

* * Instead of walking, ghosts float.

* * They never, ever open doors.

* Ghosts are only visible to kids and cats.
  Not to grown-ups. Not to dogs.

Ok – your ghost is real. Time to get **SCARY!**

* Jump out with your
most frightening face.

* Make a gigantic
monster shadow.

✱ Read spooky, creepy stories.

Your ghost might say, "Ghosts
aren't scared of *anything*!

Except . . ."

Uh-oh! *Too* scary. Help your
ghost calm down with a cup
of hot chocolate.

Promise "No more scaring!" and instead . . .

Play together!

HOW TO PLAY WITH A GHOST:

* Take turns giving
  piggybacks. Wheeeeee!

* Put on a magic show.

* Scare other people,
just a teeny bit.

WHAT *NOT* TO PLAY WITH A GHOST:

＊ See-saw. (When a ghost sits
down, it doesn't even budge.)

* Jumping on a trampoline.
(Yep – no bounce.)

* Hide-and-seek. (Ghosts
are *too* good at hiding.)

It's almost time to trick-or-treat. Your ghost probably wants a costume, too!

HOW TO CHOOSE A COSTUME:

✱ Be your favourite thing: A football.

A sparkly red robot. A banana.

✱ Be something scary: A skeleton.

A witch. A vacuum cleaner.

* Team up together and be: A traffic light.

Remember, a ghost in a costume can be seen by *everyone*. But don't worry – your parents will just think you made a new friend!

Ghosts know *nothing* about trick-or-treating,
so share your tips.

HOW TO TRICK-OR-TREAT:

✱ Don't go through doors. Knock and shout,
"Trick-or-treat!"

* Then say, as fast as you can,

THANK-YOU-VERY-MUCH-GOODBYE!

and *zoooooooom* to the next house.

* Remind your ghost not to float too high.

AARGH! No feet!

Now wish everyone . . .